E
Ca

Carlson, Nancy

Harriet's recital

HARRIET'S
· RECITAL ·

HARRIET'S
· RECITAL ·

Nancy Carlson

Carolrhoda Books, Inc. ◆ Minneapolis

for Susan Pearson, who has taught me
so-o-o much. Thanks!

Copyright © 1982 by CAROLRHODA BOOKS, INC.

Manufactured in the United States of America

LIBRARY OF CONGRESS CATALOGING IN PUBLICATION DATA

Carlson, Nancy L.
  Harriet's recital.

  Summary: Harriet overcomes her stage fright
and dances successfully and proudly at her
ballet recital.
  [1. Ballet dancing—Fiction. 2. Fear—
Fiction. 3. Dogs—Fiction] I. Title.
PZ7.C21665Has   [E]   81-18135
  ISBN 0-87614-181-5   AACR2

    3 4 5 6 7 8 9 10 91 90 89 88 87 86 85 84

Harriet loved her ballet class . . .

. . . except for one thing. Once a year the
class gave a recital. Harriet hated recitals.

"You'll do just fine, Harriet," said Miss Betty.
"No, I won't," said Harriet. "I'll trip."

All week long Harriet worried about the recital.

When she took a bath, she thought about falling.

When she saw her mother sewing her costume,

she worried that it would rip.

At last the big day arrived.

Harriet was terrified.

She knew she would never remember her
dance.

The whole thing was a big mistake.

Everyone else in her class was ready.

Miss Betty was welcoming the audience.

"I can't do this," said Harriet

as the class danced onto the stage.

"Just take a deep breath and relax," said
Miss Betty.
"I can't," said Harriet.

"On you go," said Miss Betty.

"Oh, no," said Harriet.

"Take a deep breath," Miss Betty whispered
from offstage.

Harriet took one deep breath.

Then she took another.

She took one step . . .

... then one more ...

. . . and then . . .

. . . she was dancing!

"You were wonderful," said Harriet's father.
"Were you frightened?" said Harriet's mother.
"Not a bit," said Harriet, and they all went
out for a soda.